LIZ ROSENBERG

Moonbathing

Illustrated by **Stephen Lambert**

HARCOURT BRACE & COMPANY

San Diego   New York   London

Printed in Singapore

ANYONE can go sunbathing—and often we do—but what I like best at the beach is moonbathing.

My cousin Michael says it's the perfect time to look for hidden
treasure.

Michael is so much bigger than I am that when he comes for a visit and lifts me up, I can touch my palm to the ceiling. It feels as rough as a dog's tongue. Sometimes he pays a surprise visit, arriving after bedtime. I'm happy no matter when he comes.

We only go moonbathing a few times a year. You need a clear night.
A full moon. I wear my pirate-print sweatshirt with a hood, because
moonbathing is a windy business.

By day, the beach is crowded and bright, but in the dark, the sand is cool under your sneakers. Everything turns silvery.

The sky looks like a dark ceiling pierced with holes to let the light shine through—though I know it's not really like that.

I am all set to find buried treasure gleaming under the moonlight— silver and gold, or a chest of pirate's jewels.

Across the water three lighthouses blink on and off—first white, then ruby red, then emerald, then white again.

The waves rush into shore, white-topped, spreading sideways and foaming on the sand.

They look like dancers holding hands. Moonbathing.

Once our eyes get used to the dark, we look for treasure. Michael bends down for a closer look and tosses a fan of seaweed back to sea, but he doesn't collect a thing. I find eight special pebbles, plain and speckled ones.

A piece of driftwood shaped like an X. That's the sign the pirates used for buried treasure—

so I start digging here. And, sure enough, down in the sand I find a shell big enough to capture the sound of the sea.

I wish I could take home everything I find to store in the chest by my bed.

I work for a long time, searching for more, while cousin Michael walks up and down, gazing out to sea. His white shirt glows. Suddenly he says, "Listen!"

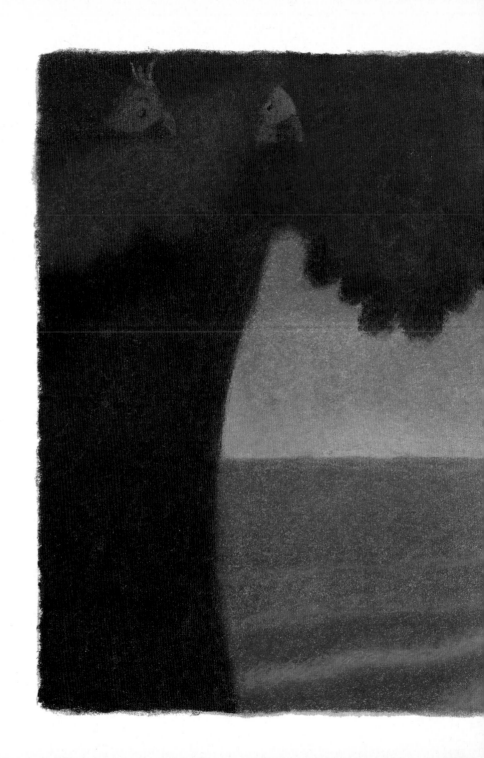

I hear a barking, like a pup. I run to Michael, forgetting about the buried treasure.

"Ahoy!" he says, pointing, then taking my hand. Something is swimming close to shore, bouncing lightly in the water like a beach ball. It lifts its head and slaps the water twice, as if to get our attention.

It is a harbor seal. Its fur is brown as a stone, with darker markings,

and its dark eyes shine like the sea.

The seal looks straight at
me for a minute—it is
moonbathing, too—then dips
under the water like a spoon
going into a bowl.

For a minute, there's no
sound at all. Then the waves
go *shhh shhh* again . . . and I'm
suddenly shivering.

Michael ties the string of my hood. He winds the scarf around my neck, and as we make the long, sweet-smelling climb back home, past beach plums and rosebushes, he picks me up and carries me.

For a minute I think if I reach up I'll be able to touch my palm to the sky, and it will be smooth as glass. I could pick hundreds of gold and silver stars and keep them in my pockets or hide them in my pirate's chest at home.

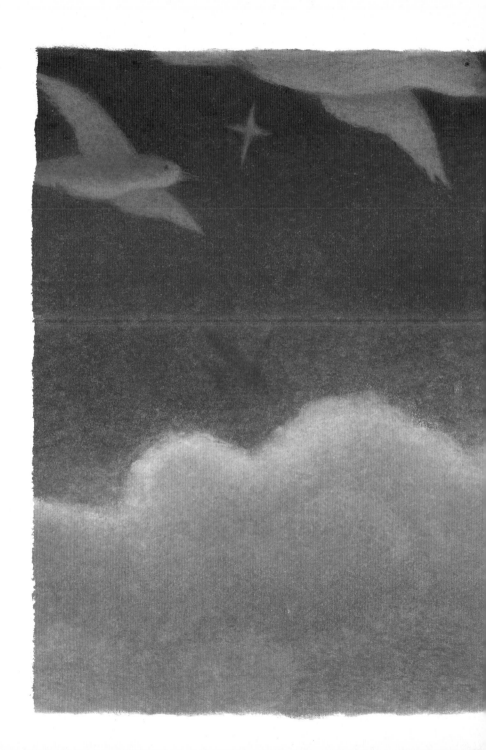

But it's better this way, all of it like this, out in the open moonlight. So I
don't even try. I'd only take them out the next time we go strolling, to put
back safe and shining, where they belong.

Moonbathing.

What you might find on your next trip moonbathing . . .

Driftwood is wood that has been carried and worn by salt water or freshwater. It often looks silvery and is smooth to the touch.

Lighthouses are usually built on rocky beaches. When fog rolls in or when there is rough weather, a lighthouse will flash strong, bright lights to ships at sea, guiding them away from dangerous areas to safety.

The moon travels around the earth every twenty-eight days, and in a year makes this trip thirteen times. When the moon is full, it can be viewed as a full circle from the earth, and can make the night seem almost as bright as day.

Oceans are large bodies of water on the earth's surface. The three oceans of the world are the Pacific, the Atlantic, and the Indian. The ocean is salty because as rainwater drains toward the sea it picks up salt from rocks and soil.

Pebbles are small pieces of rock worn smooth. They can be found almost anywhere, and some very beautiful ones are often found near the seaside. Pebbles get their soft, rounded shape from the rubbing and rushing of water against them. Some pebbles may be as old as dinosaurs.

Seaweed grows under the water, but sometimes pieces of the plant break off and wash ashore. Some are short and delicate, but others grow more than two hundred feet long and make undersea "forests." Seaweed is an important source of food and protection for the living creatures of the ocean.

Seashells have many different colors, shapes, and sizes. You can find them in the water or on the shore. If you find a large shell, put the opening to your ear and you might hear the sound of the ocean from inside the shell. What you are really hearing is the sound of your own blood moving inside your body—a different sort of "ocean."

Stars are very far away, and their light often takes years to reach us. For example, light from the second brightest star, Beta Andromedae, in the constellation of Andromeda, travels for seventy-five years before it reaches us on earth.

Tides are most noticeable when you sit by the seaside for a long time and the water creeps closer to you or slides farther away from you with each wave. Water rises and falls in the sea each day from the force of gravity. Gravity is the same force that keeps you from floating off the ground.

Waves are usually made by the rising and falling of tides and from weather such as winds and storms. You can see small waves caused by breezes and large waves caused by high winds.

Seals are sea animals with bodies that look a bit like a dog's but with flippers instead of legs. They belong to the same animal family as dogs, called mammals. People are mammals, too.

Most seals live in oceans or inland seas and spend most of their time in the water. Some, like the harbor seal in *Moonbathing*, also spend time on land. The harbor seal belongs to an earless group of seals. This doesn't mean they don't have ears; it just means we can't see them easily. Harbor seals are also found more often on land or on floating chunks of ice than other seals. They tend to be rather shy around people.

Seals live along the coast of North America from southern California to Alaska, as well as in the Northeast from the mid-Atlantic to the North Pole.

I wrote this book about a beach on Cape Cod. A visit to the beach is the best place to find out more about the ocean. But to learn more about marine mammals and the ocean and how you can help keep the world of marine life safe, you can also visit your local aquarium or write: Greenpeace, Public Information, 1436 U Street NW, Washington, DC 20009. Also available is a young person's newsletter, called Kid's Alert, *issued by Greenpeace.*

This book is dedicated to our son, Eli, my happy childhood
near the Long Island Shore, and to Cape Cod.
—L. R.

To Jack and Nancy
—S. L.

Text copyright © 1996 by Liz Rosenberg
Illustrations copyright © 1996 by Stephen Lambert

Requests for permission to make copies of any part of the work should be mailed to:
Permissions Department, Harcourt Brace & Company, 6277 Sea Harbor Drive, Orlando, Florida 32887-6777.

Library of Congress Cataloging-in-Publication Data
Rosenberg, Liz.
Moonbathing/Liz Rosenberg; illustrated by Stephen Lambert.—1st ed.
p.   cm.
Summary: A young girl relishes the magical atmosphere of the beach at night
when she goes for a moonlit stroll with her older cousin.
ISBN 0-15-200945-0
[1. Beaches—Fiction. 2. Night—Fiction. 3. Moon—Fiction. 4. Cousins—Fiction.]
I. Lambert, Stephen, 1964–   ill. II. Title.
PZ7.R71894Mr   1996
[Fic]—dc20   95-18490

First edition
A C E D B

The illustrations in this book were done in chalk pastels on paper.
The display type was set in Chanson D'Amour.
The text type was set in Bell.
Color separations by Bright Arts, Ltd., Singapore
Printed and bound by Tien Wah Press, Singapore
This book was printed with soya-based inks on Leykam recycled paper,
which contains more than 20 percent postconsumer waste
and has a total recycled content of at least 50 percent.
Production supervision by Warren Wallerstein and Ginger Boyer
Designed by Linda Lockowitz